40325

D0515720

About the Book

ANIMAL LENDING LIBRARY said the sign. Isn't that nice! Stephen thought. A place where animals can take out books.

But it turned out that this was a library which lent animals to children instead of books.

During the next few weeks Stephen thought about nothing else except how he could borrow a small brown rabbit.

His adventures make a charming, simply written story that will delight younger readers.

JEAN FRITZ writes: "Young readers will be interested to know that there really are Animal Lending Libraries in many parts of the country. My own daughter is campaigning for a local Animal Lending Library. Her own preference, however, would be not to read a rabbit but a fawn."

About the Author

Jean Fritz, her husband and two children live in Dobbs Ferry, New York, where Mrs. Fritz devotes most of her spare time to writing.

How To Read A Rabbit

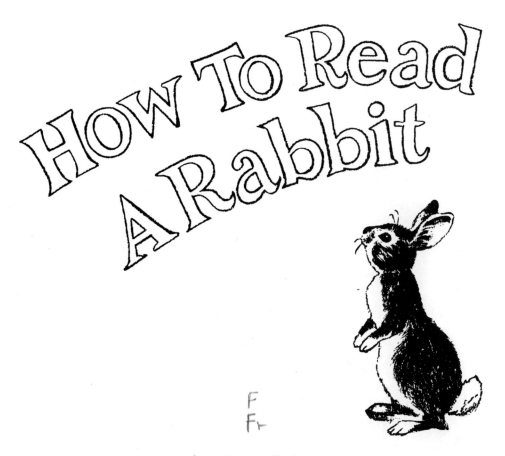

by Jean Fritz

illustrated by Leonard Shortall

Coward-McCann, Inc.　　　　　New York

To Lee

Library of Congress Catalog Card Number: 59-11433

Ninth Impression

Manufactured in the United States of America

One day after school, instead of going straight home Stephen took a long, winding, dillydally way that went past the Junior Museum. He walked slowly and kicked a stone in front of him for a while. He ran a stick along the top of a hedge for another while.

When he came to the Museum, he stopped.

There was a new sign hanging above the side door of the museum. The sign had a picture of a mouse on it, a picture of a squirrel, and an arrow pointing toward the door. There were three words on the sign, but Stephen, who was six years old and in first grade, could read only the first word.

Animal, it said.

Stephen smiled. "Isn't that nice! They have a special door for animals to use."

And he sat down on the steps to wait for the animals to come.

He planned just how it would be.

Stephen waited and waited. But no squirrels came. No mice. Not even any dogs or cats.

Instead, after a long time, a boy came. He was a high school boy with books under his arm and as he came near, Stephen stood up and cleared his throat loudly.

"Say," he said to the boy, "about that sign up there. Could you tell me what it says?"

"Sure," the boy answered. "Animal Lending Library." And he opened the door and went inside.

Stephen sat down on the steps again. "Animal Lending Library," he repeated. "*Animal Lending Library!*"

"Isn't that nice!" Stephen said. "A place where animals can take out books."

And he planned just how it would be.

Maybe there would even be a rabbit. Of all the animals in the world, Stephen liked rabbits best. He closed his eyes and planned for a little brown rabbit with a tiny, tiny book in his mouth.

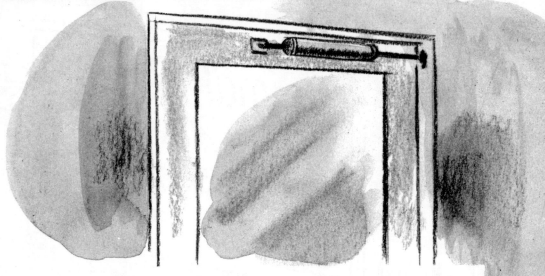

When he opened his eyes, there was no rabbit. As a matter of fact, there were no animals at all.

And Stephen had waited long enough. He stood up and walked through the door where the arrow pointed.

The first thing he saw was a tall desk with a librarian sitting behind it. The desk was like the one downtown in the library for people where he took out books. The librarian seemed to be the same kind of librarian and she was working with the same kind of cards. Stephen wondered if the rules in both libraries were the same. He remembered the rule in the downtown library—*No Animals Allowed in the Children's Room.* He hoped there was no rule here — *No Children Allowed in the Animals' Room.*

If there was such a rule, nobody told him. Stephen turned away from the desk to see what an Animal Lending Library really looked like.

But all Stephen could see in the room was crates. There didn't seem to be any animals and there wasn't a single book.

Stephen put his hands on his hips. "Say," he said loudly, "what kind of a library is this?"

The librarian smiled. "It's an animal library," she explained. "We lend animals to children instead of books. A boy or girl can take an animal home and keep him for a week and then return him for someone else to take out."

Stephen stepped forward and then he saw that the crates weren't really crates at all. They were cages. And inside every cage there was a pair of bright eyes looking out.

"Isn't that nice!" Stephen said. *"Isn't that nice!"*

There were all kinds of animals in the library. There was a field mouse named Mickey, a snake named Sleuth, a squirrel named Cashew, and an owl named Goggles. There was a tame, de-perfumed skunk named Magnolia, who could sit up on her hind legs and beg. There were three hamsters, two guinea pigs, a cageful of white rats, and a beehive in a glass box.

Stephen had walked all the way around the room before he noticed that over in one corner there was a cage he had missed. He went back to see it. Hanging out of the wire netting in front of the cage was a piece of green lettuce.

Inside the cage there was a brown rabbit.

Stephen picked the cage up by the handle and walked straight to the librarian's desk.

"I'd like to take out this rabbit," he said.

The librarian hesitated. "What's your name?" she said.

"Stephen Wilcox."

"You don't have a card, do you, Stephen?" the librarian asked.

Stephen shook his head. "No."

"How old are you?"

"Six years old," Stephen answered loudly, "and I have had my own card at the library downtown for a year."

The librarian smiled. "I'm sorry, Stephen," she said, "but at this library you have to be seven years old. There are other rules too. After you join, you have to work in the library and take care of the animals for at least two months before you can take one out."

Stephen looked down at the brown rabbit whose nose was twinkling against the wire cage. Slowly he carried the cage back to its corner and slowly he walked out of the library.

When Stephen reached home, he found his brother, Kenny, who was eleven years old, mowing the front lawn.

"Hi," Kenny said. "What are you looking so glum about?"

Stephen kicked his toe into the ground. "You'd look glum too," he grumbled, "if you were only six years old."

"Could be," Kenny admitted and he went on mowing. He pushed the mower up to the end of the lawn. Then he turned around and came back and walked past Stephen in the other direction. Stephen wished he would stop and talk.

"You know what?" Stephen said.

"What?" The grass flew out from behind the blades of the mower.

"They have a new room at the Junior Museum."

"Yea?" Clickety-clack, clickety-clack.

"They lend out animals," Stephen shouted above the whir of the lawn mower. "You can take one home for a week."

"Uh-huh."

Stephen tried again. "Not just regular animals," he said. "They lend out skunks and snakes and squirrels."

At last Kenny stopped mowing. "Are you kidding?" he asked.

"No. Honest."

Then all at once, as Stephen looked at his brother, he had an idea.

"You could join," he said. "There's a little brown rabbit there." Stephen began to talk very fast. "You could bring her home and I'd take care of her for you."

And Stephen planned how it would be.

The next day Kenny joined the Animal Lending Library. For two months after that he went to the library every day to learn how to take care of the animals. Stephen went along and watched Kenny clean out the cages and feed the different animals.

Earthworms for the snake, acorns for the squirrel, meat for the owl, pellets for the hamsters and guinea pigs, cereal and celery for the white rats, and dog food for Magnolia, the skunk, whenever she sat up and begged.

And lettuce and carrots for the brown rabbit in
her cage in the corner.

Then one day the librarian told Kenny that he had had enough practice taking care of the animals. He had his permission slip signed by his mother saying he was allowed to bring animals home.

So, the librarian said, Kenny could borrow an animal any time now that he wanted to. Today even.

"Good!" Kenny said. "There's a Scout meeting at school this afternoon and I'll take an animal along with me."

He started walking around the room, looking at all the cages, trying to decide which animal he would take.

Stephen stood in the corner of the room beside the rabbit cage.

"Take the rabbit, Kenny," he said. "Remember how we planned it. Please take the rabbit, Kenny. Please."

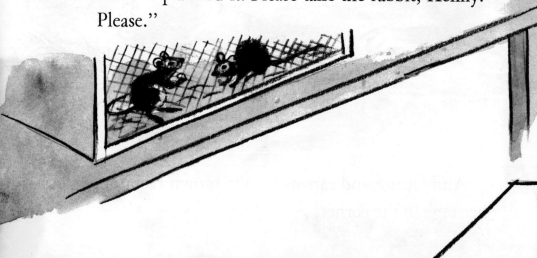

But Kenny didn't go near the corner with the rabbit cage.

"I never said I'd bring the rabbit home. That was your idea," Kenny said. "I want to take an interesting animal to Scout meeting. An animal that can *do* something."

Kenny stopped in front of the skunk's cage. "Like Magnolia," he said. "A trick skunk that begs! That's better than an ordinary dumb little rabbit."

"Rabbits aren't dumb," Stephen shouted. "They're nice. Take the rabbit home and you'll see how nice she is."

Kenny didn't pay any attention. He picked up the skunk's cage and took it to the desk to have it stamped out.

Then he looked down at Stephen's long face. "I tell you what," Kenny said. "You can carry the cage to the Cub Scout meeting for me all by yourself. Just as if you were seven years old and it was your skunk. I'll go home, change into my uniform and meet you at school."

A skunk wasn't as nice as a rabbit, of course.

It wasn't what Stephen had planned.

Still, a skunk was nice to have when a boy like Butch Edwards came along. Butch was a big boy and fond of fighting. Stephen met him in front of the school.

"Set down that crate, kid," Butch growled when he saw Stephen. "Set it down, I said."

Stephen set down the crate as he was told. But his knees didn't shake as they usually did when he saw Butch Edwards. Instead, Stephen smiled to himself. He unfastened the lid on the cage and lifted Magnolia out in his arms. He stroked the white stripe that ran down the middle of Magnolia's back. He fluffed out the fur on her tail.

"You know what trick Magnolia can do?" Stephen asked.

Butch's eyes were as big as two baseballs. He didn't wait to hear what Magnolia could do.

Magnolia didn't wait to hear what she could do either. No sooner had Butch disappeared than Magnolia decided to disappear too.

Before Stephen could put her back in her cage, Magnolia tensed her four legs, wriggled herself loose from Stephen, and jumped onto the top step of the school. Through the open door she ran and into the school itself.

Stephen raced after her—through the long corridor, down the steps to the basement, and into the furnace room where Mr. Bean, the janitor, was reading the paper. Mr. Bean jumped into the coal bin as Magnolia dashed past him and streaked out the other door, up the steps again and to the first floor, with Stephen still behind.

Magnolia ran past the closed door of Stephen's first-grade room, past the closed door of the second-grade room, past the closed door of the third-grade room, then through the open door of—the principal's office.

Mr. Cane, the principal, was sitting at his desk and he didn't see Magnolia when she first came in. The first time he had any idea there was something strange going on was when an arithmetic workbook suddenly fell off the bookcase.

Mr. Cane looked up and there was a skunk on the bookcase, pushing workbooks deliberately onto the floor, one after another.

Mr. Cane was a very smart man. He knew that a skunk is most dangerous when frightened.

So, in order not to frighten the skunk, Mr. Cane sat still and watched Magnolia push over all the workbooks, upset a vase of roses, knock down a bottle of ink, and chew up a third grade spelling list.

All the time, Stephen stood out in the hall watching, afraid to come in. One by one, the Cub Scouts, arriving for their meeting, joined Stephen quietly in the hall.

When Magnolia had finished on the bookcase, she hopped up on Mr. Cane's desk, sat on her hind legs, dangled her front paws in the air and begged.

The trouble was that Mr. Cane didn't know she was begging. He didn't know *what* she was doing or *what* she planned to do.

Stephen moved into the doorway. "She's hungry," he explained in a small voice.

Mr. Cane didn't seem to understand. Hardly raising his eyes from Magnolia, he told Stephen to stop where he was. He talked slowly with long, electric spaces between his words.

"Go out quietly," he said. "Tell Mr. Bean to call the S. P. C. A." He was a smart man and knew what to do in emergencies.

Stephen started to do as he was told because, after all, Mr. Cane *was* the principal. Still, he didn't do exactly as he was told. First he went to Mr. Cane's desk.

"I'll just take Magnolia with me," he said quickly. "She's from the Animal Lending Library."

When Kenny arrived at the Cub Scout meeting, Magnolia was back in her cage and Stephen was sitting in the chair always reserved for the guest of honor.

"You should have been here!" the boys said to Kenny. "You missed it. Mr. Cane thought Magnolia was wild. You should have seen his face when Stephen picked her up. You should have seen how Stephen did it. Man, was it ever great!"

Stephen felt unusually tall sitting in his chair and almost as if he, himself, were wearing a Cub uniform like Kenny's with badges up and down his sleeve.

When Kenny and Stephen got home, they took Magnolia up to their bedroom. Kenny set the cage down on the floor and opened it.

"Don't touch her," Kenny said. "Let's just watch what she does."

Magnolia came out of her cage slowly and
looked at the strange room as if she weren't quite
sure that she could trust it. She sniffed at the
wastepaper basket; she peeked under the beds.
She walked toward Kenny's desk. On the floor in
front of the desk was the small black bear rug that
Kenny's father had given him for Christmas. The
head of the bear was at one end of the rug and it
stared at Magnolia.

Magnolia's fur prickled up stiff as porcupine quills. She looked into the open mouth of the bear and she took a careful step forward. The bear didn't move.

She took another step.

Still the bear didn't move. He didn't even blink his black beady eyes. He just grinned at Magnolia with his two rows of sharp white teeth as if he dared her to come closer.

Suddenly Magnolia jumped up on her front legs so that her hind legs and tail were waving high in the air. She looked as if she were doing a handstand.

"Isn't that interesting!" Kenny cried. "That's the position a wild skunk takes when he shoots off his perfume. Magnolia's acting as if she were still wild. *Isn't that interesting!*"

"You know what I'm going to do?" Kenny said. "I'm going to keep a notebook the way scientists do. I'll call it 'Interesting Facts about Interesting Animals.' I'll write down everything I observe—first about Magnolia and then about all the other animals I bring home."

Kenny rummaged in his desk and found a notebook he could use.

It was such a thick notebook that Stephen didn't like to look at it. He didn't want to think about all those empty pages that had to be filled. He closed his eyes and tried to remember his plans. But all he could see was a long line of "interesting" animals streaming into the house and not a rabbit among them. No matter how tight he squeezed his eyes, he couldn't see a single rabbit.

Every day Kenny wrote his observations down in his notebook—when Magnolia ate, how much she slept. He made a list of the things that pleased Magnolia, such as bananas, and the things that displeased her, such as bear rugs and vacuum cleaners and wind-up toys.

While Kenny made notes, Stephen made crosses. Every day he crossed off another day on the calendar. On the day that Magnolia was due at the library, Stephen counted up the number of days that were left until his seventh birthday.

"One hundred and eighty," he counted, "one hundred and eighty-one, one hundred and eighty-two." When he had finished counting, he found that he had two hundred and three days to wait.

After they returned Magnolia to the library, Stephen went straight to the rabbit's corner.

"I wish you could learn to do something interesting," Stephen whispered to the rabbit. "If you don't, Kenny will never bring you home."

If only she could learn to stand on her head, Stephen thought. Or sit up and beg. Or turn a somersault. Stephen closed his eyes and planned all the things a rabbit might do.

When he opened his eyes, the rabbit was just sitting still, being brown.

The librarian was talking to Kenny. "Have you seen our new pet?" she asked. "We have a flying squirrel that came in last week. His name is Zorro. Maybe you'd like to take him home today."

Stephen looked back sadly into the rabbit cage. One thing was certain. No matter how hard she tried, a rabbit would never learn to fly.

The whole family gathered in the basement playroom to watch Zorro come out of his cage. Stephen tried to imagine a squirrel flying around the room like a bird, waving his short legs up and down and maybe steering with his tail. Would he go right up like a helicopter, he wondered, or would he need a running jump?

Zorro didn't seem eager to take off. He ambled out of his cage, walked lazily over to a sofa at one end of the room and jumped up on it.

"What's he jumping for?" Stephen asked. "I thought he was supposed to fly."

Zorro jumped up to the back of the sofa.

"Huh," Stephen snorted. "I bet he's just a regular squirrel."

Zorro jumped still higher onto some shelves. Then once more up to the top of a window, where he clung to the curtain rod and blinked down at his audience.

Then all at once Zorro spread his four legs wide and sprang into the air. The skin around his legs seemed to unfold and stretch until he looked like a fur kite with eyes sailing through the air. He skimmed and soared and glided down to the ping-pong table.

"Did you see that!" Kenny cried. "He doesn't really fly; he glides. Isn't that *interesting?*"

For one week Kenny measured Zorro's glides and wrote down the distances in his notebook.

"Rabbits jump pretty far," Stephen told Kenny. "You could measure a rabbit's jumps."

Kenny did not seem interested.

When the time came to take Zorro back, Stephen did not even go along. Instead, he stayed home and waited. When Kenny came back, empty-handed, Stephen met him at the door.

"Well, where is it?" he asked. "Is it invisible or something?"

"I didn't bring one home," Kenny said. "I'm in that swimming meet at the park and I knew I wouldn't have time. I'll wait a couple of weeks."

Stephen felt his face grow fiery red. "You could have brought me the rabbit," he said.

Kenny looked surprised. "You know, I didn't even notice it."

When Kenny was ready to go back to the library, his mother reminded him that Aunt Martha would be arriving that night. "You know how nervous Aunt Martha is," Kenny's mother said. "Please don't bring back anything that will frighten her. Pick a gentle animal."

Stephen smiled. Maybe, after all, he thought . . . maybe . . . This time he would go along.

When they got to the library, Stephen stayed close to Kenny.

"Remember Aunt Martha," Stephen said when Kenny stopped in front of the snake's cage.

"Remember Aunt Martha," Stephen said when Kenny looked at the beehive.

Stephen guided Kenny safely past the white rats.

Now they were almost to the rabbit corner. They had only the owl's cage to pass. Goggles, the owl, would, of course, be sleeping as usual, crouched in a dark corner, looking more like a brown feather duster than a bird. Surely not even Kenny could think a feather duster was interesting.

Today, however, Goggles wasn't quite asleep. The upper parts of his eyes were closed as usual, but the lower parts were open into slits that looked like new crescent-shaped yellow moons.

"I'd like to see him at night," Kenny said, "when his eyes are wide open. I bet he looks great." He looked thoughtfully into the cage.

Already it seemed to Stephen that he could see Goggles at home in a dark room. He saw the two yellow slit eyes opening to half-moon eyes and then wider and wider until there were two full moons glowing in front of him. He could even hear Kenny talking about how interesting Goggles was. Then all at once Stephen seemed to hear something else—a long, ghostlike noise in the dark.

Whoooo-ooooooooh

Stephen took Kenny's arm. "Owls hoot at night," he said. "They make scary noises and Aunt Martha wouldn't like them."

Stephen steered Kenny quickly to the rabbit corner.

At last.

But the rabbit cage was not there. The table where the cage always stood was empty. Bare, flat, and empty. Stephen stood in front of the table and stared at the emptiness.

"Someone else must have taken out the rabbit," he whispered to himself. He started to picture the rabbit at someone else's house but he didn't like the picture. He started to picture his own house without the rabbit and he didn't like that picture either.

Stephen didn't notice the librarian coming across the room until all at once there she was, standing in the rabbit corner between Kenny and Stephen, smiling. Stephen wished she would stop smiling. He wished she would go away.

"I have something new to show you boys," she said gaily, motioning for them to follow her.

Probably a flying toad, Stephen thought crossly. He shuffled along behind, carrying all the emptiness of the rabbit corner along with him.

The librarian unlocked a door at the back of the library and they went into a room filled with boxes and file cabinets and old furniture.

"Wait here just a minute," the librarian said, still smiling, "and I'll bring back a surprise."

Stephen didn't want to see any surprises. He didn't even want to see the librarian. When she came back with a cage in her hands, he dropped his eyes and stared stubbornly at the floor. He heard Kenny draw in his breath, and he knew what Kenny would say before he said it.

And Kenny did. "Isn't that interesting?" he
said.

"Stephen," the librarian said, "you might like
this too."

At last Stephen looked up.

There in the cage in front of him was the brown rabbit he knew so well. Beside the brown rabbit were five baby brown rabbits.

For a moment Stephen couldn't find any words.

Then he smiled. "Oh, isn't that nice!" he whispered. *"Isn't that nice!"*

"They're two weeks old," the librarian said, "and have just opened their eyes. I thought Kenny might like to take the whole cage home."

The librarian looked at Stephen. "How long is it until your birthday, Stephen?"

Stephen didn't look up. "One hundred and seventy-six days."

"Well, I don't know what to do," the librarian said. "The library can't possibly take care of all these new rabbits. I wonder, Stephen, if you'd like a birthday present one hundred and seventy-six days ahead of time. Would you like one of these babies for your own?"

Slowly Stephen looked up. "To *keep*?" he whispered.

"To keep."

Right away Stephen began to plan how it would be.

When Stephen and Kenny got home, they opened the cage and sat down on the playroom floor to see what would happen.

One by one, the five baby rabbits came out and began to explore. They took tiny, little hops in one direction, tiny, little hops in another direction, and then tiny, little hops back to the mother rabbit.

But the smallest, brownest rabbit hopped in one direction only. He went straight to Stephen and hopped into his open hand.

Stephen picked him up. "This one is mine," he said.

Kenny opened his notebook. "You know," he said, "I believe the rabbits are going to be the most interesting of all."

And everything was just as Stephen had planned it would be.